DATE		
APR 0 4 1995	JUN 0 6 2001	
MAY 1 0 1995	JUN 2 8 2001	
JUL 1 8 1995	JUL 1 8 2001	
AUG 1 1 1995		
AUG 2 5 1995		
OCT 1 3 1995		
NOV 1 4 1995		
APR 2 5 1996		
JUN 0 4 1996		
MAY 2 1 1997		
JAN 1 3 1998		
AUG 1 5 1998		

This book has been

donated through the

Friends of the Library

Redbud Gift Fund

ZERO GRAVITY

BY Gloria Skurzynski

Winner of the American Institute of Physics
Science Writing Award

BRADBURY PRESS   New York
Maxwell Macmillan Canada   Toronto
Maxwell Macmillan International
New York   Oxford   Singapore   Sydney

Nonfiction by Gloria Skurzynski

ALMOST THE REAL THING
Simulation in Your High-Tech World
GET THE MESSAGE
Telecommunications in Your High-Tech World
HERE COMES THE MAIL
KNOW THE SCORE
Video Games in Your High-Tech World
ROBOTS
Your High-Tech World

Bradbury Press
Macmillan Publishing Company
866 Third Avenue
New York, NY 10022

Maxwell Macmillan Canada, Inc.
1200 Eglinton Avenue East
Suite 200
Don Mills, Ontario M3C 3N1

Macmillan Publishing Company is part of the Maxwell Communication Group of Companies.

First edition
Printed in Singapore by Toppan Printing Company on recycled paper
10 9 8 7 6 5 4 3 2 1
The text of this book is set in Futura.

Library of Congress Cataloging-in-Publication Data
Skurzynski, Gloria.
Zero gravity / by Gloria Skurzynski.—1st ed.
p.   cm.
Includes index.
ISBN 0-02-782925-1
1. Gravitation—Juvenile literature.   2. Weightlessness—Juvenile literature.
[1. Gravity.   2. Weightlessness.   3. Astronautics.]
I. Title.
QC178.S49   1994
531'.14 dc20   93-46735

A highly focused text and full-color photographs give an understanding of gravity's effects by
comparing and contrasting what happens in zero gravity—as on a space shuttle flight—with a
young reader's experiences with gravity on Earth. The scope of *Zero Gravity* is intentionally
restricted to a discussion of effects within the Earth's gravitational field.

The picture on page 9 is a simulation created by the author to illustrate
Galileo's law of falling bodies.

This book is dedicated
to the men and women of NASA,
who are heroes of this century and the next.

ACKNOWLEDGMENTS

The photographs on pages 4, 6, 8, 11, 12, 15, 20, and 29 are by Gloria Skurzynski. Warmest thanks to models Kathy Ferguson, Tom Thliveris, Anthony Lopez, and the students at Sycamore Elementary School in Crowley, Texas. All other photographs courtesy of the National Aeronautics and Space Administration, with special thanks to Mike Gentry and his staff at NASA/Johnson Space Center in Houston, Texas, and Manny Virata and his staff at NASA/Kennedy Space Center at Cape Canaveral, Florida. The author is extremely grateful to Noel de Nevers, Ph.D., and aerospace physicist Phillip Novak for reviewing the text of this book for accuracy.

The author would like to acknowledge the astronauts who appear in the photos from NASA included in *Zero Gravity*: Mae Jemison, Endeavor, p. 16 • Mark Lee, Endeavor, p. 17 • Mamoru Mohri, Endeavor, p. 19 • Tamara Jernigan, Columbia, p. 21 • George Nelson, Discovery, p. 22 • Loren Shriver, Atlantis, p. 23 • Norman Thagard, Challenger, p. 24 (top) • Rhea Seddon, Columbia, p. 24 (bottom) • David Hilmers, Discovery, p. 25 • Marsha Ivins, Atlantis, p. 26 • Andrew Allen, Atlantis, p. 27 • Richard Richards, Columbia, p. 28 • Bonnie Dunbar, Columbia, p. 28

When you jump on a bed, why don't you fly up to the ceiling and stay there? What makes you sink back down onto the mattress?

It's a force called gravity.

What makes gravity work? No one is absolutely sure. But we do know many things about gravity. Earth's gravity pulls everything toward the center of the Earth. It works on balls, and waterfalls, and feathers.

"Gravity doesn't work on a helium balloon," you might say. "If my little brother's balloon escapes, it goes up, not down."

That's because the helium in the balloon weighs less than the air around it. As long as the balloon doesn't stretch or leak, it will rise higher and higher, until it reaches thin air that weighs the same as helium. Then it will stop rising. Earth's gravity will keep the balloon from floating into space.

Earth's gravity is felt far away, even farther away than
our moon, which is about 240,000 miles from Earth.
Our moon is held in its orbit by Earth's gravity.

More than three hundred years ago, a young student saw an apple fall from a tree to the ground. His name was Isaac Newton. Before his twenty-fourth birthday, Newton figured out that the apple fell to Earth for the same reason our moon stays above the Earth. The reason is gravity.

All objects have a gravitational pull on one another, Newton stated. The amount of pull depends on how far apart the objects are, and on how much mass each one has. The greater the mass, the greater the pull.

Mass means the amount of matter in a thing. On Earth, matter takes up space and has weight.

Earth has such a huge amount of mass that its gravity attracts everything that comes near it—as close as an apple, as far away as the moon.

Always, Earth's gravity pulls everything toward the center of the Earth. All objects fall toward Earth at the same speed, no matter how big or heavy they are. Another scientist—Galileo Galilei—discovered that fact before Newton noticed the falling apple.

If there were no air resistance to slow things, two sky divers could toss a ball back and forth as they fell. (Of course, there's no way to skydive without air, and where there's air, there's air resistance. But if there were a way. . . .) It wouldn't matter that the divers were bigger and heavier than the ball— they would all fall together.

This is called *free fall.* It means that the divers and the ball are falling at the same speed, pulled down by gravity.

So why doesn't our moon fall to Earth like an apple? Or a sky diver?

Have you ever ridden on a roller coaster with a 360-degree loop? As you speed around the loop, gravity is pulling you toward the ground. But at the same time, speed on a curved path creates a centrifugal effect that pushes you outward, away from the center of the loop. That's what centrifugal means: "flying away from the center."

As long as the coaster cars move fast enough, you won't fall out, even when you're upside down. The centrifugal effect crams you against your seat. It's stronger than the pull of gravity.

The moon's velocity (forward speed) as it orbits Earth creates a centrifugal effect that is equal and opposite to the pull of Earth's gravity. That effect makes the moon stay in its path, and not fall to Earth.

Try whirling a ball at the end of a string *very* slowly. It will wobble and sag downward. If you whirl it fast, you'll feel the centrifugal pull of the ball as it travels around the center—your hand. The faster you whirl it, the stronger the pull will be, and the ball will stay up off the ground.

Think of your hand as the Earth and the ball as the moon. Because Earth's gravity is pulling on it, the moon doesn't fly away. At the same time, the moon's forward motion pushes it away from the center (Earth) and keeps it circling. This centrifugal effect balances the force of gravity.

The faster you whirl the ball, the stronger the centrifugal effect becomes. If you suddenly let go the string, the ball will fly away until gravity brings it back down.

If you whirl it even faster before you let it go, the ball will fly even farther before it falls back to the ground.

If you could whirl that ball to a super-swift speed—more than seven miles per second—and then let it go, it would soar into space and completely escape Earth's gravity. Space shuttles don't go that far because they don't go that fast.

It takes a lot of force to thrust a heavy space
shuttle to the right speed to orbit the Earth. Hot gases
from burning rocket fuel shoot down, pushing the shuttle
skyward. To reach orbit, the shuttle must be lifted to an
altitude of about 200 miles above the Earth's surface and
must reach a velocity of about 17,500 miles per hour.

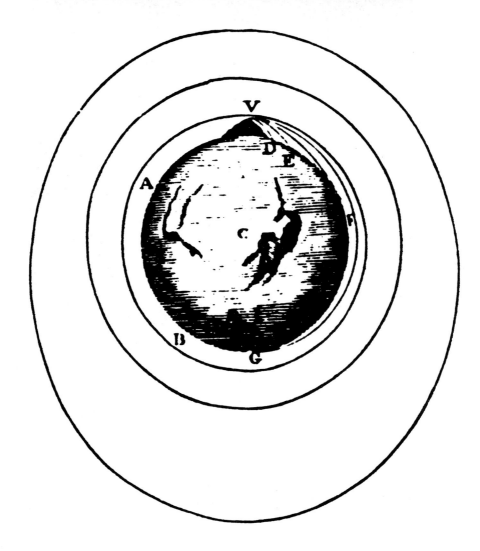

Isaac Newton wouldn't have been surprised that shuttles orbit the Earth today. In 1687, he published a picture of a cannonball orbiting Earth.

Shoot the cannonball, Newton said, from a mountaintop above the Earth's atmosphere, where there is no air to slow it. It will fall to point *D*. Shoot it faster, and it will fall to point *E*. Keep increasing the speed it is fired at, and it then will reach points *F* and *G*. Finally, you'll shoot the cannonball so fast that the curve of its fall will match the curve of Earth's surface. It will fall all the way around Earth and be in orbit.

When an object orbits Earth, gravity pulls on it, making it fall back toward Earth. But it never lands, because as the object falls in an arc toward Earth, the Earth's surface curves around in the same direction. The object's path is parallel to Earth's spherical surface.

As long as nothing changes the object's forward speed—and in the vacuum of space, there's nothing to drag on it—it will keep circling Earth. It will be in orbit.

Space shuttles orbit the Earth. Other spacecraft, though, are sent out farther, to explore our solar system. These space probes usually orbit Earth a time or two; then special rocket boosters fire to give them an extra push. This speeds them up so much that they soar into deep space, *beyond* the pull of Earth's gravity.

Space shuttles, though, always stay in orbit. *Space shuttles never—ever—travel beyond the pull of Earth's gravity.* Two hundred or so miles above Earth, the pull of gravity on a shuttle is almost as strong as if the shuttle were still on Earth. It's the shuttle's orbiting velocity that causes a centrifugal effect that balances the pull of gravity. That balance makes the shuttle seem weightless.

The shuttle and its contents fall together at the same speed around Earth. The astronauts don't feel as if they're falling. They feel as if they're floating. Like the sky divers with the ball, they're in free fall. Unlike the sky divers, they won't land on Earth—the astronauts will just continue to fall around Earth as long as the shuttle stays in orbit. This state of continuous free fall is called weightlessness, or microgravity, or zero gravity. Or it's just called zero-g.

Zero-g does *not* mean that gravity doesn't affect the shuttle. It just means that the effects are mostly canceled out by centrifugal force.

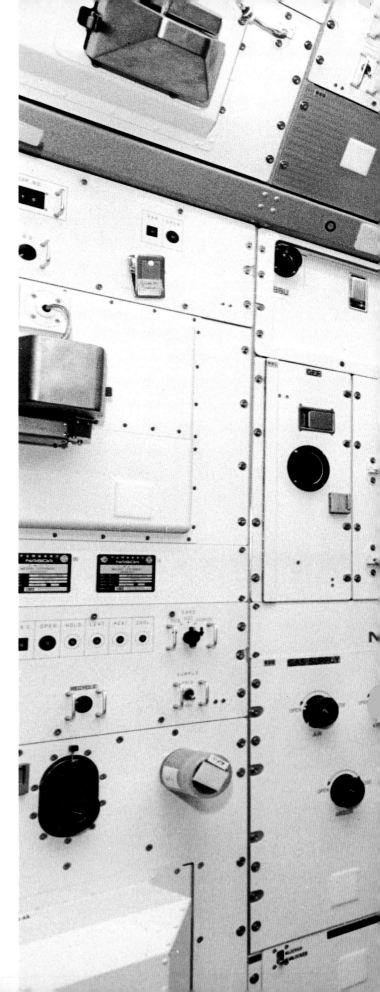

Imagine that you're an astronaut inside an orbiting space shuttle. Imagine you're holding an apple up in front of you. You let go of the apple and then lower your arm.

Since you and the shuttle and the apple are all in free fall, all falling around the Earth at the same speed, the apple won't move in relation to you. It will stay still in the space around you. The apple is falling around the Earth just as the moon is falling around the Earth. So are all the astronauts, the shuttle, and everything else inside the shuttle.

Everything feels weightless.

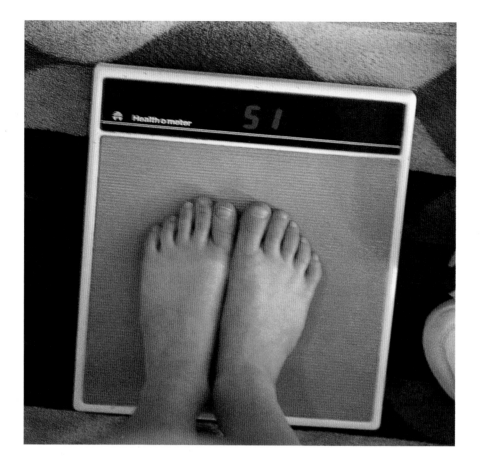

Does *weightlessness* mean you can't get weighed in space? That's exactly what it means.

On Earth, at one-g, you can step on a scale. Since gravity is pulling you toward the center of the Earth, your weight squeezes the springs inside the scale. The heavier you are, the harder the springs get squeezed, and the higher the numbers go to show you how much you weigh.

In zero gravity, if you stood on a scale, nothing would happen. There'd be no force of gravity to pull you down. Since astronauts can't get weighed while they're in orbit, they measure their body mass instead.

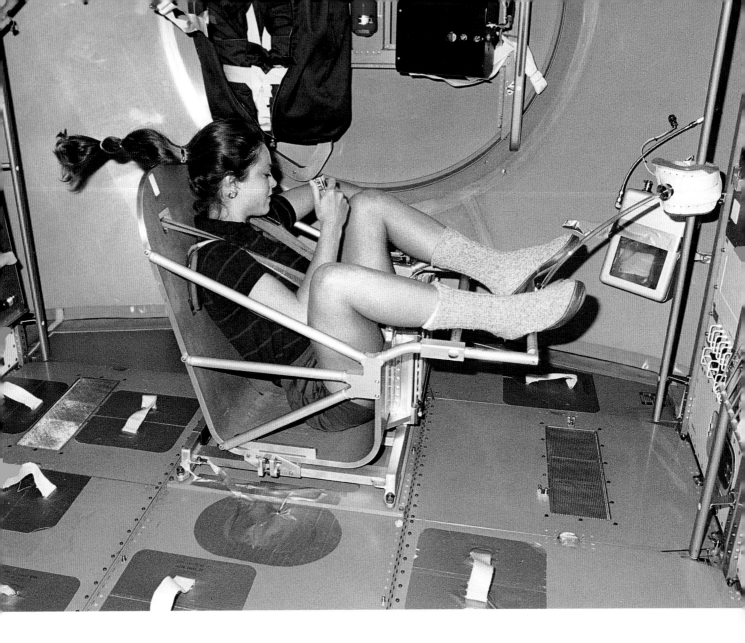

In orbit, astronaut Tammy Jernigan has to strap herself into the body-mass measuring device so she won't float away while she's being measured. Tammy Jernigan enjoys zero-g. She says: "I think of it as falling around the Earth. It's a very free and joyous feeling. Weightlessness makes some of the most tedious tasks pleasant. Things that were heavy and difficult to move around on Earth are quite maneuverable here in zero-g."

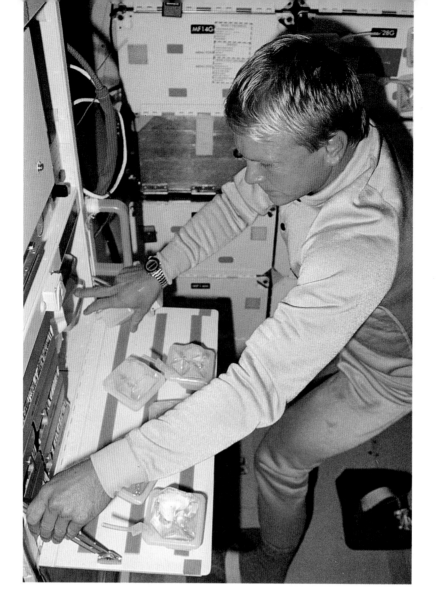

Zero gravity can get messy.

Whenever an astronaut opens a locker or a pocket, loose objects float out and drift around the cabin.

At mealtimes, astronauts have to hold on tight to their silverware. All of the dishes and beverage containers have Velcro on the bottom so they can stick to the Velcro strips on the countertops.

To keep from floating around while they're eating, astronauts slip their feet into loops on the cabin floor.

Astronauts have been known to play with their food—it happens on almost every shuttle flight. It's tempting to toss up a couple of pieces of candy and then watch them slowly glide into your open, waiting mouth.

Anything soft and gooey, such as pudding, must be pressed firmly onto the spoon. Otherwise, it can end up on a wall or in the ventilation system.

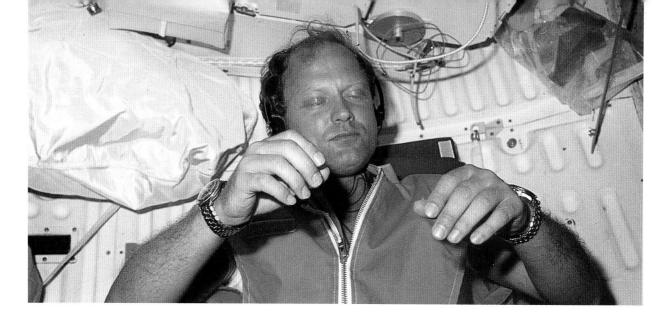

In space, sleeping is an unusual experience, too. Since there's no up or down in zero-g, astronauts can stretch out in any direction, wherever there's room. Straps keep them from drifting. Because their arms aren't usually strapped in and because there's no gravity to hold them down, the arms tend to rise above the sleepers, making them look ghostlike.

On a space shuttle, a bunk bed is just a padded board with an attached sleeping bag. No mattress is necessary, because a weightless body doesn't press down: Weightlessness makes you feel as if you have the softest imaginable pillow and mattress beneath you.

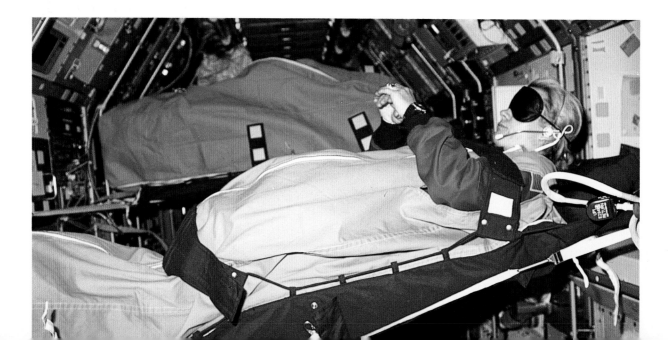

Space shuttles don't have chairs—astronauts don't need them. In zero-g, people just naturally go into a semi-sitting position, without even thinking about it. They look like they're sitting on invisible furniture.

Astronauts sometimes fall asleep when they're supposed to be working. Usually, no one notices, because the astronauts' heads don't nod forward and because their weightless bodies don't slump. Although their muscles relax, anything they're holding stays in their hands, since there's no gravity to pull things from their unclenched fingers. The only clue that they're asleep is their closed eyes.

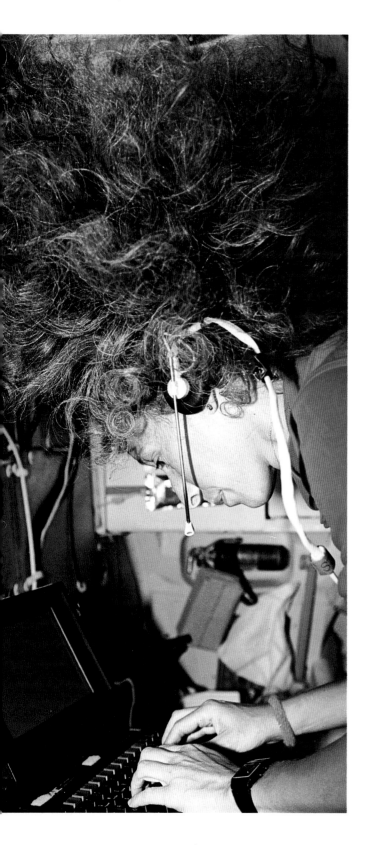

While traveling in space, astronauts *look* different. In the absence of gravity, their body fluids move up toward the chest and head; this makes their faces puff up and their cheeks go higher. Hands swell, too.

Also, humans stretch in space. Since the spine is no longer compressed by gravity, it becomes longer. During shuttle missions, some astronauts have grown two or almost three inches taller! But as soon as they return to Earth's surface, they lose those extra inches of height.

And in zero-g, long hair needs to be held in place by a cap, a clip, or a ribbon. Otherwise, it goes completely wild!

Some body changes are harder to see.

The human body was made to live with gravity. Starting from the day of your birth, you needed about a year to learn to balance upright. Your bones and muscles, and tendons and ligaments all work to support your weight against gravity's never-ending pull toward the center of the Earth.

Take away that pull, and the bones and muscles have less work to do. Bones grow weaker; muscles shrink. Since shuttle missions rarely last longer than two weeks, this weakening isn't serious—astronauts always exercise during a mission, to stay fit and strong.

Still, they keep careful records of their bone and muscle losses in space. What they learn will help other astronauts, on the much longer voyages of the future.

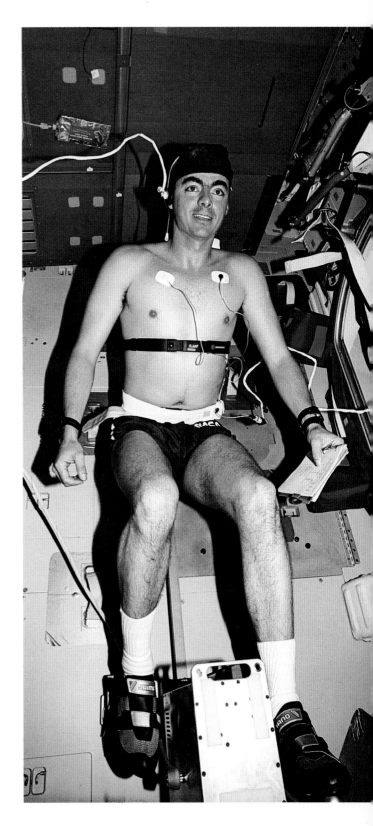

With each shuttle mission, astronauts learn more about living in zero gravity.

Will weightlessness ever seem normal to humans? Probably not.

Joseph Allen, one of the astronauts who flew on a space shuttle mission says, "Zero gravity is so bizarre that even if [the inside of a shuttle] looked like your mother's house, it doesn't feel like your mother's house, because you float. Floating is so extraordinary!"

Never for a single moment, the astronaut says, are you fooled into thinking you're on Earth.

On Earth, you almost never forget which way is up. Or down.

You may feel a little unsure on a roller coaster, or when ocean waves tumble you underwater. Or during a fast spin on the gym bars. Those feelings last only a few seconds.

Very quickly, gravity reminds you where you are.

GLOSSARY

acceleration the rate at which speed or direction changes

air resistance drag; the force that slows the motion of a body moving through air

altitude the height of an object above Earth's surface

atmosphere all the air surrounding Earth

body a portion of matter

centrifugal force the apparent force that makes a rotating body move away from the center of rotation

force a push or pull on an object; the strength or energy that changes the shape or motion of a body

free fall motion caused by gravitational forces alone

Galileo Galilei Italian astronomer and physicist, born 1564, died 1642. He made precise studies of motion.

gravitation the force that attracts every particle of matter to every other particle of matter in the universe; also, the attraction of objects to one another due to their masses

gravity the force that tends to draw all bodies in the Earth's sphere toward the center of the Earth. Beyond Earth's sphere, gravity extends throughout the entire universe.

helium a very lightweight gas. Because it is not flammable, it's used to inflate balloons.

mass the amount of matter in body. Mass determines how the body will accelerate due to force applied to it.

matter anything that occupies space. Three kinds of matter are liquids, gases, and solids.

microgravity 1: The condition of free fall. Albert Einstein concluded that there is no physical difference between free fall and the absence of gravity.
2: *Micro* means "one-millionth." The additional forces, such as atmospheric drag, that influence an orbiting shuttle, amount to about one-millionth of Earth's gravity.

Newton, Sir Isaac English mathematician, born 1642, died 1727. He made major discoveries in mathematics and in the science of optics, and developed the law of universal gravitation.

orbit the path of a body through space. An orbit is usually curved. A space shuttle goes into orbit when the force of gravity pulling it down toward Earth is balanced by the forces pushing it up and ahead.

planetary explorer a spacecraft that leaves Earth's field of gravity to orbit or fly past our sun's planets

solar system our sun, the nine planets that orbit it, and the satellites of those planets

space the universe outside Earth's atmosphere

vacuum a space completely empty of matter

velocity the rate of motion of a body in a particular direction

INDEX